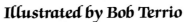
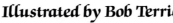

Look and Find

Peter Rabbit

The Tailor of Gloucester
Two Bad Mice • Mrs. Tiggy-Winkle
Ginger and Pickles • And more!

Illustrated by Bob Terrio

Cover illustrated by Bob Terrio and Jerry Tiritilli

Illustration Assistant: Gale Terrio

Illustration script development by Jane Jerrard

Louis Weber, C.E.O.
Publications International, Ltd.
7373 North Cicero Avenue
Lincolnwood, Illinois 60646

Manufactured in the U.S.A.

8 7 6 5 4 3 2

ISBN 1-56173-417-9

PUBLICATIONS INTERNATIONAL, LTD.

Peter Rabbit was a naughty little bunny! He disobeyed his mother and went straight to Mr. McGregor's garden. He wasn't alone, though!

First, look for Peter. Then look for his friends who joined him in Mr. McGregor's garden.

Peter Rabbit

Benjamin Bunny

Jemima Puddle-Duck

Squirrel Nutkin

Mrs. Tiggy-Winkle

Jeremy Fisher

Tom Kitten

Hunca Munca

Hunca Munca and Tom Thumb decided that this dollhouse was much nicer than their mouse hole. They packed up their mouse belongings and moved right in!

Can you find these things that the mice are using in their new home? Can you find where Peter Rabbit is hiding, too?

Peter Rabbit

A postage stamp

A bottle cap

A chess piece

A domino

A toothbrush

A thimble

A crayon

When Jemima Puddle-Duck met the foxy gentleman, she was nearly duck soup! Peter Rabbit would have told her to stay in her own backyard.

Can you find Peter? Can you find Jemima and her farmyard friends? Look for these funny farm things, too!

Peter Rabbit

Jemima Puddle-Duck

Rebeccah Puddle-Duck

Kep

"Kid" gloves

A pig "pen"

A cow "belle"

A "horse shoe"

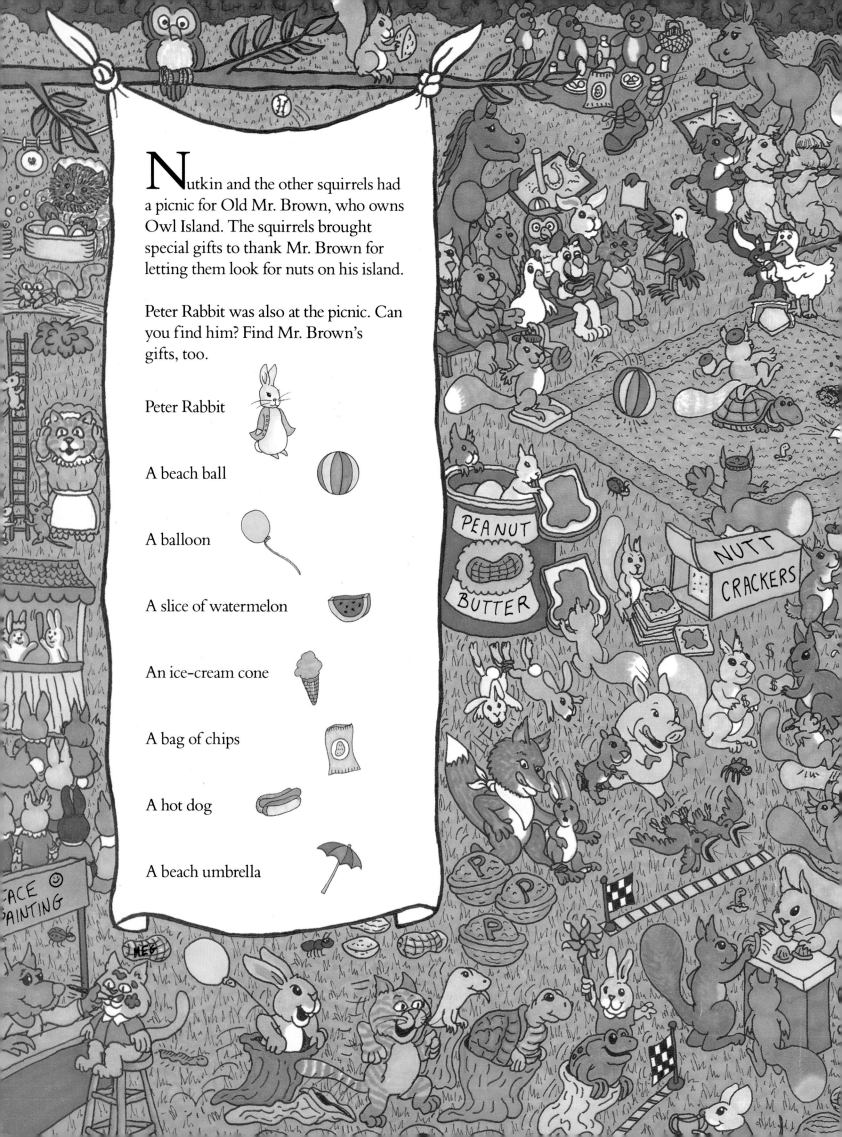

Nutkin and the other squirrels had a picnic for Old Mr. Brown, who owns Owl Island. The squirrels brought special gifts to thank Mr. Brown for letting them look for nuts on his island.

Peter Rabbit was also at the picnic. Can you find him? Find Mr. Brown's gifts, too.

Peter Rabbit

A beach ball

A balloon

A slice of watermelon

An ice-cream cone

A bag of chips

A hot dog

A beach umbrella

The tailor of Gloucester fell ill before he could finish the Governor's fancy Christmas coat. But the coat was mysteriously finished Christmas morning! Who were the tailor's helpers?

Peter Rabbit knows. He was visiting the shop that night! Can you find him? Can you find these things for sewing?

Peter Rabbit

A pincushion

A thimble

A dressmaker's dummy

A pair of scissors

This button

A measuring tape

This spool of thread

Ginger and Pickles are having a big sale! Peter Rabbit has found a good bargain on garden tools. Jemima Puddle-Duck is hoping to buy a new bonnet.

After you find Peter Rabbit and the store owners, look for these customers who have come from farm and field for this once-a-year event.

Peter Rabbit

Ginger

Pickles

Squirrel Nutkin

Hunca Munca

Jemima Puddle-Duck

Jeremy Fisher

Mrs. Tiggy-Winkle

It's a beautiful morning, and Benjamin Bunny is on his way to see Peter Rabbit. Benjamin and Peter end up in all kinds of trouble by the end of the day.

First, find Peter and Benjamin. Then look for these other things from *The Tale of Benjamin Bunny.*

Peter Rabbit

Benjamin Bunny

Tabby cat

Mrs. McGregor's bonnet

Peter's jacket

A red handkerchief

A tam o'shanter

Mrs. Rabbit's knitting

DIAPER SERVICE

MRS. TIGGY-WINKLE'S WASH-O-RAMA

Mrs. Tiggy-Winkle does such a good job of washing and ironing, Peter Rabbit has helped her start a business! The animals now bring her all their dirty laundry.

First, find Peter Rabbit. Then look for these things that need washing.

Peter Rabbit

Peter's jacket

Cock Robin's vest

Lucie's pinafore

Sally Henny-Penny's stockings

Mrs. Rabbit's handkerchief

Tabby Kitten's mittens

Jeremy Fisher's raincoat

ALTERATIONS

LET OUT

CAT'S PAJAMAS

EMPEROR'S NEW CLOTHES

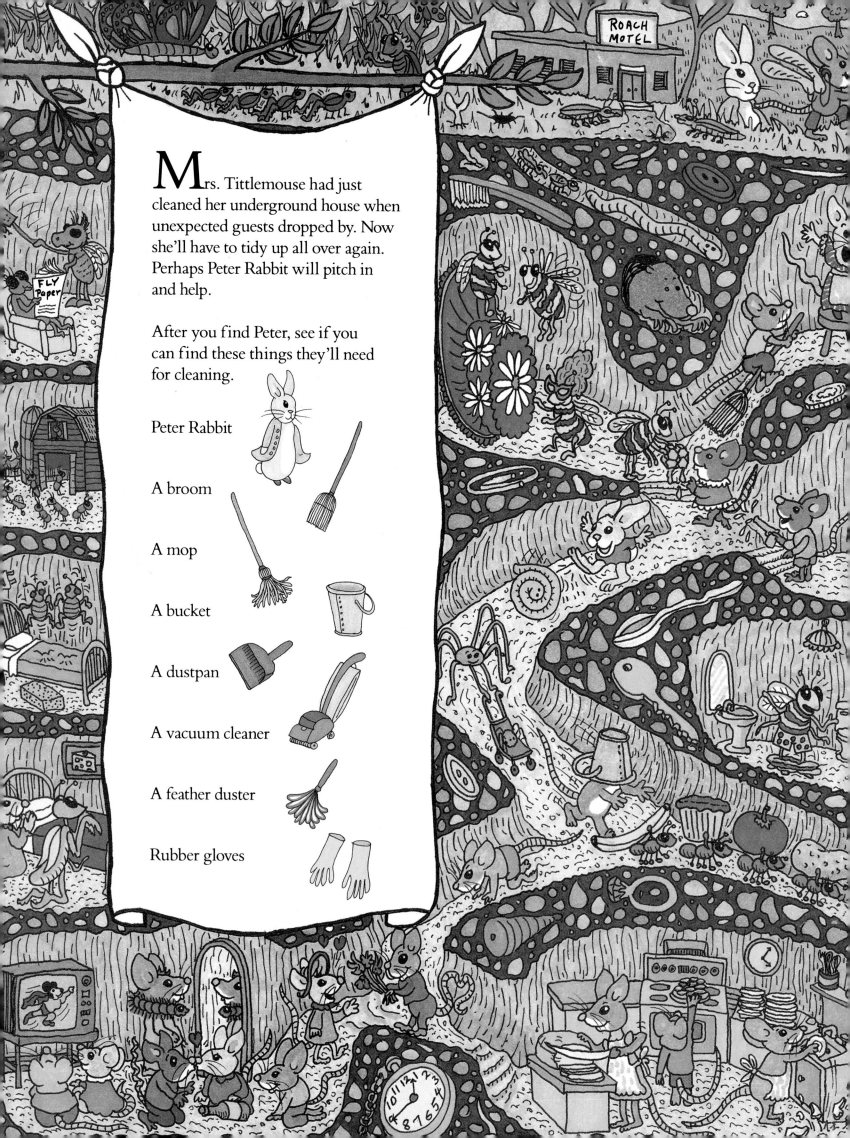

Mrs. Tittlemouse had just cleaned her underground house when unexpected guests dropped by. Now she'll have to tidy up all over again. Perhaps Peter Rabbit will pitch in and help.

After you find Peter, see if you can find these things they'll need for cleaning.

Peter Rabbit

A broom

A mop

A bucket

A dustpan

A vacuum cleaner

A feather duster

Rubber gloves

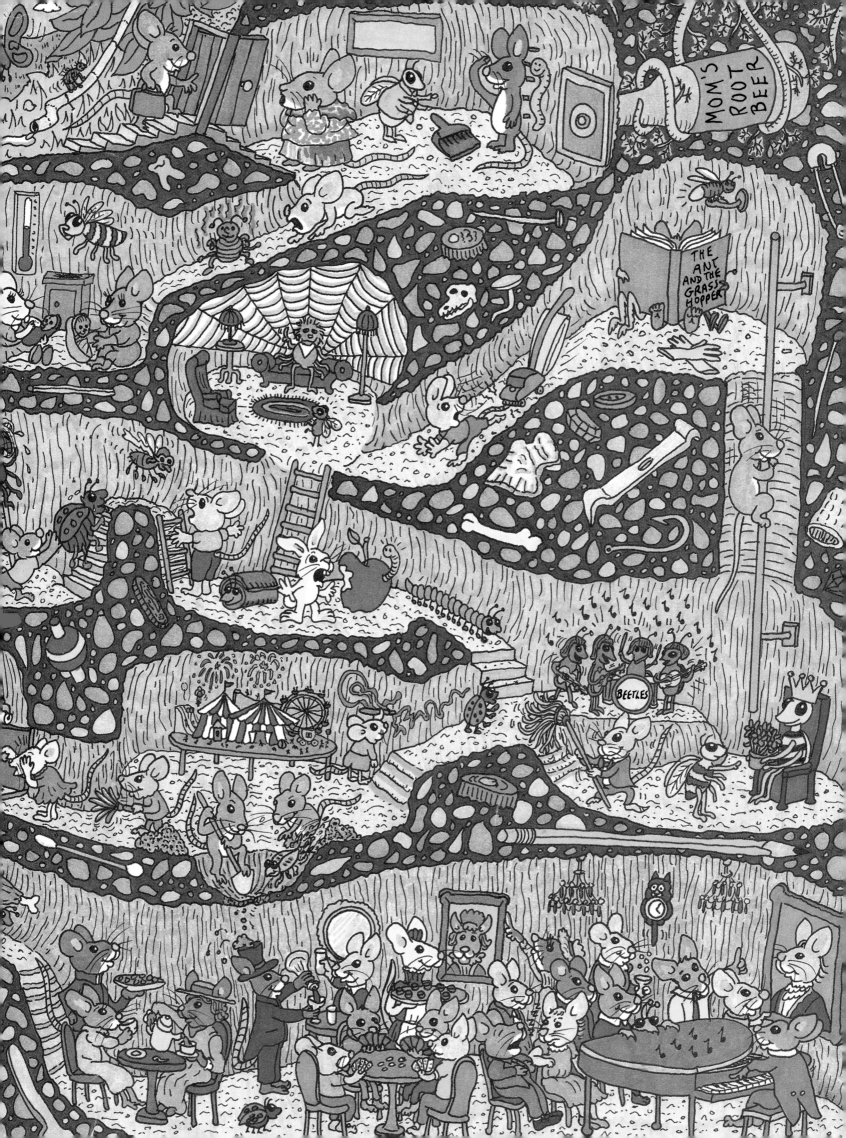

The bad mouse-children never put away their things. Can you find these mouse toys in the dollhouse?

- ☐ A teddy bear
- ☐ A red wagon
- ☐ A spinning top
- ☐ A beach ball
- ☐ A tricycle
- ☐ Roller skates
- ☐ A ballerina doll
- ☐ A dump truck
- ☐ A robot

Go back to the tailor's shop. Other than the tailor mice, can you find these mice?

- ☐ A tinker mouse
- ☐ A soldier mouse
- ☐ A spy mouse
- ☐ A church mouse
- ☐ A "right-field" mouse
- ☐ A mailmouse
- ☐ A mouse who's stirring
- ☐ A repairmouse

Turn back to Jemima's farm to look for these "fowl" things.

- ☐ A lucky duck
- ☐ A wild-goose chase
- ☐ A Christmas goose
- ☐ A turkey dinner
- ☐ A sitting duck
- ☐ A "chicken" chicken
- ☐ A hen-pecked husband

Go back to the Owl Island picnic to search for these nutty things.

- ☐ Nuts and bolts
- ☐ Nutmeg
- ☐ Cold, hard "cash"-ews
- ☐ "Wall"-nuts
- ☐ "P-cans"
- ☐ Brazil nuts
- ☐ "P-nuts"
- ☐ Spanish peanuts
- ☐ Nutt Crackers

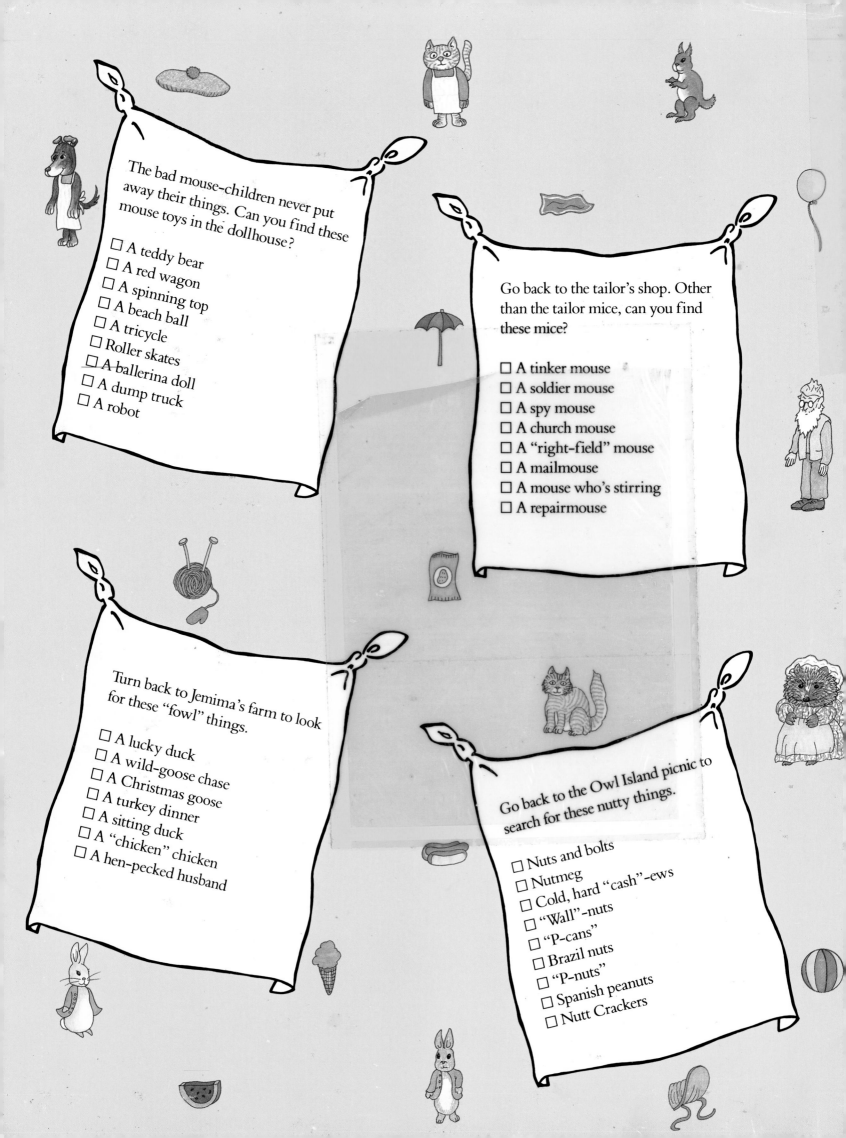